THE CHARON EXPRESS

Dylan Ritch

For Liv,

The girl who believes androids can love, Sci-Fi is a forward reflection of the soul, and the promise of redemption belongs to everyone.

It was not the gentle vibration from beneath or the blinding white light from above that woke the man, though both were present. It was not the sterile smell that burned his nostrils or the texture of cured leather beneath his hands. No, it was guilt that lulled him from his sleep. A sleep he did not remember entering. Guilt pried open his eyes, admitting the harsh beams that caused the man to lift his left hand and shield himself.

When his sight finally adjusted to the colors and shapes around him, the first thing he noticed was the silver band around his left ring finger. The precious metal quickened his pulse and dropped his jaw.

"Welcome to the Acceptance section," said a hollow voice that buzzed as it spoke.

The man dropped his hand and let out a considerable gasp.

In front of him sat a robot with glossy vanilla skin made of hard plastic and a body shaped like a mannequin. On its chest was a circle, the size of dinner plate, consisting of intricately laced panels.

From there, plastic shoulders formed upward into the shape of a hood, a dark screen filling the space where a face should be. Inside that void, a neon blue ring illuminated the center of the glass. The man regarded that it looked like a giant pupil-less eye.

He went white in the face and jerked back, halted by the soft cushioned seat in which he sat. Slowly, he took stock of his strange surroundings.

Around him were the makings of a bullet train unlike any he'd ever seen. The walls, seats, and tables were clinically clean, something you did not see in the city. As a result, every move the man made produced an audible squeak. A red latex suit compressed itself against every inch of his body, leaving only his hands and face free.

4

He pulled at the burgundy saran wrap but found no zipper or release to peel it off, only a thin empty pocket on his right thigh. The robot sat across from him, waiting for a response.

"Where am I?" he asked.

"You're aboard the Charon Express," the robot replied.

A small, round, silvery table hovered between them, blue energy pulsing from underneath it. The man peered beneath the table, dumbfounded. He felt as if he'd landed in the middle of a science fiction film. Across the aisle, on the man's left, was an identical seating arrangement. Two pairs of white seats faced each other, with the same floating table between them. There were four of these pods in the train cart, including his own. Every one empty except for his. This did nothing for the man's nerves.

The top of robot's blue eye caved in toward the center of the circle. To the man, the robot looked like a confused cyclops with a unibrow.

"What's a Charon Express?" the man asked.

The robot brought its hands to the edge of the table. Tiny black magnetic balls conjoined its wrists and fingers along with every other joint in its body.

"You don't know?" it inquired.

The man's sweaty palms gripped the armrests, producing the loudest squeak yet.

"I, uh, I think I hit my head."

It was not a lie, but not a truth either, more like a reasonable possibility the lost fellow could not confirm or deny. A way to enjoy the comfort of deception without the shame of lying.

"Then I will provide medical attention," the robot offered, preparing to stand.

"Oh no, it's not that serious. I'm just having a hard time remembering how I got here."

If, at this moment, the man could have been granted one wish, it would have been to be a more proficient liar. The glossy figure leaned forward and paused.

"You don't remember why you are on this train?"

The man climbed out of his seat and escaped to the aisle with cautious steps backward. He shook his head. The robot committed another dreadful pause, escalating the man's perspiration problems.

"May I see your ticket, sir?"

It stood.

With a silent prayer, the man patted the pocket on his thigh. As expected, he found nothing.

"I seem to have misplaced it."

It was now the robot's turn to take a step back.

"You don't have a ticket?"

The robot delivered each word slowly. Its blue eye widening to the edges of its dark face. The man continued running his hands over the suit in a futile attempt to find another hidden pocket. Eventually, he admitted to himself that no amount of wishful thinking could materialize a ticket he did not have. He smiled an apologetic, toothy grin of apprehension and shook his head no.

"Fascinating." the robot said, "Absolutely fascinating."

The man swallowed hard. The guilt was still there but subsided against his growing fear of the strange artificial being before him.

"What are you?"

The robot straightened and reached out a slender hand.

"I'm your conductor," it said and stepped forward.

The man did the only thing the man could do.

The man ran.

Abandoning curiosity for safety, he scrambled down the train cart to a circular door behind him. To his relief, it opened at his approach. Beyond was a tiny hallway, no bigger than four feet. He burst through it, to the next coach, and skidded to a stop.

Inside was the making of a stable; a mix of dirt and straw covering the floor. On either side stood stalls with large Clydesdales hanging their muscled necks over the doors. In the center of the stable was a woman wearing a suit identical to his own, carrying a basket of apples. Her red hair rested on her right shoulder in a ponytail, giving a clear view of her heart-shaped face. Forest green eyes blinked at him from above a button nose. He was so stunned by her presence that he almost didn't notice another robot standing beside her.

The basket fell from the woman's hands, apples scattering in all directions.

"Peter? Is that the real you?" she said.

The robot beside her recovered from its shock much faster than the woman.

"You are not permitted to be on this train," it said, extending a hand to the man.

The magnetic joints that made up its arm disconnected and floated in the air. Bright blue electricity arced between the suspended pieces and reassembled them into a cannon. This same blue lightning gathered in the cannon's bore and took aim at the man's chest.

The man, now designated as Peter, screamed. His terrified yell crescendoing in sync with the powering of the blue laser beam.

"AHHHHHHH!"

The cannon blasted a humming ball of blue light toward him. A gust of hot wind passed over the man's right cheek as another identical blue ball came from behind, meeting with the one in front. The collision caused an explosion that sent him flying backward into the stiff arms of the Conductor.

"Back to the cart," the Conductor said, dragging him back through the hallway.

The original robot dragged him through the transition hallway, the door closing behind them as they reentered the white room.

"What the hell is going on?" Peter yelled.

He pushed the Conductor away and backed himself against a wall, his fingers accidentally pressing a slick touchscreen panel that slid the wall upwards. A flood of fearful adrenaline unlocked some latent athletic ability inside Peter. He leaped into the air, higher than he could ever remember jumping. The opened wall revealed a window where outside swirling nebulas and gases created a kaleidoscope of color amidst the vastness of space.

Peter turned to the Conductor, turned to the window, turned back, and screamed again.

"Peter. We should sit," the Conductor said.

It sat in the pod across from him and gestured to an empty chair. Peter gave the mesmerizing terror beyond the window a parting look before shuffling over to the seat offered him. He plopped down and let out a wavering sigh.

"I must ask you to not interrupt as it will only complicate—" the Conductor began.

"I think I'm allowed a few freakouts after almost being vaporized, thank you," Peter retorted.

His body demanded a fight-or-flight response, and so far, flight had done him no good.

The Conductor shrugged at him, which Peter could not help but think looked rather silly on its stiff shoulders.

"You are on the Charon Express, which, for the sake of simplifying, is a train that takes you to the afterlife."

"THE AFTERLIFE!"

"This is the interruption complication I was referring to earlier. Yes, the afterlife. The oddity is that only one person is supposed to be aboard the Charon at a time. After seeing that woman with the Recognition Conductor, I can conclude she is the rightful passenger and not you. Combine that with your lack of a ticket, and we can safely deduce you are a stowaway. The first to ever board the Charon. As programming dictates, every Conductor on this train, apart from me, will try to kill you."

Peter crossed his arms. "May I talk now?"

The Conductor, who had been orating with his animatronic fingers, dropped them onto the table.

"Is that what you're focusing on? The fact I asked you to be quiet? You were almost murdered just now, and I'm promising there will be more attempts in the future."

"Crazy can only pack a punch for so long. You said you're bringing me to the afterlife. Doesn't that mean I'm dead? How can I be killed if I'm dead?"

"The word killed was used to promote easier understanding. To speak more accurately, you'd be erased. Deconstructed, atom by atom, to the point your consciousness would cease to exist."

The Conductor began rubbing its glossy finger against the silver table as it spoke. It created a ringing note, like someone rubbing the wet rim of a glass. Peter found it most annoying.

"The real question is if you died, and she died, then what went wrong that led to you both being here?"

"She's dead too..."

This realization shook Peter to his core. His heart sat in his chest like a hundred pound weight.

She was dead too, and he was on the same train as her...

Thinking of her flushed his cheeks. The way she looked so serene amongst those horses, the warmth in her eyes, and most notably, the way his name sounded in her voice.

He spun the mysterious wedding ring on his finger.

"Do you know who she is?" Peter asked.

"She is the rightful passenger. When a person dies, they board their unique version of the Charon. They traverse the Recognition carts until they are ready to meet me here, in Acceptance, where I take them to see the Engineer, who designates their placement based on a review I give of their actions while alive."

The Conductor continued its ringing during this explanation.

"What's in the beyond?" Peter asked while putting a hand up to his ear.

Ring…Ring…

"I would melt if I tried to tell you. Goes against my programming."

"Of course it does."

Ring. Ring. Never-ending ring!

"Could you stop!"

Peter grabbed the Conductor's hand and grimaced at its cold and slick touch.

"If it pleases you," the Conductor said, taking its hand back and resting it on a knee.

"You said the other conductors would try to kill me, but not you. Why?"

"Again, programming. The Engineer stations one Conductor for each half of the Charon. One for Recognition and one for Acceptance. We wait for the passenger to appear. When they do, we assist them in their journey until they are placed. You appeared in my cart, Acceptance. That makes you my passenger. Programming demands I help you. But you also don't have a ticket which initiates my programming's want to destroy you. To speak colloquially, I have very mixed feelings about you."

Peter glowered at the Conductor and threw his hands in the air.

"Okaaaayyy. Where does that leave us?"

The Conductor took yet another long pause, which at the very least, Peter preferred over the ringing.

"I'm going to follow my programming," the Conductor said.

It stood and walked to the circular door opposite the one the man had run through. Peter got the idea he was supposed to follow. They passed through another transition hall before entering a room filled with a bright orange ball of fire. A heat wave stole the air from Peter's lungs and sent him into a dizzy spell.

It was a simple but large room with no distinct factors aside from a wide window behind the orb that looked out into space. The burning globe stood at around twelve feet and pulsated as if at any moment it could explode. Peter diverted his eyes to keep from being blinded by the miniature sun.

"What is that?" he asked.

"This is the engine room, and that is the Charon's power source. The Engineer. The consciousness that initiated the Big Bang, as humans call it. It generates the massive amount of energy necessary for powering the Charon and dictates all placements."

"What's the room made of? Freaking Solar panels?"

The Conductor pointed to a hole in the floor below the Engineer. Several ring devices spread out from the hole's edge. The orb swayed but never moved outside the outermost ring. The rings were white, just like the Conductor, with the same blue energy glowing from periodic sections of black glass.

"The conduits suck in the excess energy from the Engineer, and use it to power the entire train, even us conductors."

Peter scratched the back of his head.

"So, what happens now?"

"Normally, I would provide a report on you and then the Engineer would place you in the proper afterlife. However, I do not have the necessary data to make my report. To remedy this, I'm going to send you back to the Recognition carts with me to review your life. I will rewrite the system to believe you are the real passenger. This will deter the Recognition Conductor from trying to kill you. To a point."

"Woah, robo! To a point? So your twin is still going to try and murder me?"

"Certainly. That's why I'll be going with you and temporarily acting as your Recognition Conductor. You need only walk through the memory, replaying your actions as they happened on Earth. This way, the real Recognition Conductor won't be able to distinguish you from the rest of the simulation."

Peter shifted his feet, putting his hands to his hips.

"What if I'm having a hard time remembering what happened when I was alive?"

The Conductor leaned forward at the waist.

"Do your memory problems persist that far?" it asked.

Peter stretched his arms out wide.

"I don't know what to tell you. What happens to the woman I just saw? She's still on the train."

The Conductor straightened.

"Your memory problems will present a critical complication, but my hypothesis is that the process of Recognition will help restore them. Do you know the woman?"

"I feel like we have to be connected somehow."

The Conductor narrowed its eye.

"I will work the woman into the system. Should you and her share any memories, she will play her part accordingly. She was already nearing the end of the Recognition section so I will have adequate data for her placement."

"So you're what? Taking over her mind?"

"It is not so invasive. She would simply reenact her memories like you. The difference is by designating you as the prime passenger and her as a part of the simulation, the system will freeze her should the memory be altered. Be warned, should you go against the memory, the Recognition Conductor will find and eradicate you."

Peter scoffed, "Then why the hell should I go?"

"Because failure to do so will force me to enact my secondary programming, which is to eradicate you."

The Conductor's arm disassembled just as the other had.

"Okay! Okay! I get it. You're the sheriff in these parts," Peter said. "I'll try to remember, I guess."

"That would be most helpful," replied the Conductor, turning its hand back to normal and bringing it to the circular panel on its chest.

The panel retracted into its body to reveal a glowing blue crystal. Its glow magnified, shooting a streak of blue lightning at the orange orb. The energy of the Engineer and Conductor collided, sparking against each other.

At first, Peter worried the sun ball might explode. But as he watched the lighting and space magma interact, he came to suspect they were actually communicating. The room shifted as the blue and orange powers crackled against each other. Everything around him entered a slow motion. Light and matter distorted, stretching the room forward. The walls, the cosmos outside, the Conductor, and even his own body became overexposed. A elongated and distorted phantom of himself extended out before him. The only thing that did not warp was the orb.

He barely had the time to recognize the strange phenomenon before the connection severed, sending the blue beam racing back into the Conductor's chest with a loud pop. All the overexposed light shot back into position like a stretched rubber band correcting itself. The returning force flung Peter backward. Light and color raced past him so fast that he couldn't discern where or how far he'd traveled. When the universe finally stopped, he rolled onto his knees, dry heaving.

"You couldn't have warned a fella?" he spat.

"I was unaware you'd be so negatively affected. I've never traveled between carts with a passenger before."

Peter stumbled to his feet, assessing whether his insides were still a part of his body.

"So, we're in a memory cart now, right?"

"Correct! The first one!" said the Conductor, pointing a metal finger in the air.

"Oh, excited I figured it out, huh? I'm not dumb."

Peter took stock of the cart, which, like the last, was not a cart at all but a restaurant with stringed Edison bulbs across the ceiling and fake vines hanging from the rafters. Tables and chairs fashioned from dark wood with ornate carvings spread across the room. Peter drew a sharp breath when his eyes came across an intimate table set for two.

"Do you remember anything?" the Conductor asked.

"Something, yeah. Just like a gut feeling." Peter said.

The Conductor dropped his finger with a clank against his side.

"I suppose that would have been too simple."

The restaurant was packed with customers, frozen in mid-conversation. Not a soul moved while the room held its breath.

Waiting.

The only seats left were at the bar and the empty center table where two candles sat on either side of a preset bottle of red wine. A theory, a hope rather, crawled its way into the back of Peter's mind.

"This is the kind of place you take someone special. Like on a first date, or an anniversary, or a proposal."

His feet guided him to the table in small steps.

"Did you take someone special here? Someone who affected the trajectory of your life?" The Conductor asked.

Peter turned to the Conductor and held up his left hand.

"I could have, couldn't I? I mean, look at this ring! I was obviously married, and I bet you my wife was the same woman who's your real passenger. Maybe we both died at the same time and accidentally got put on the same train, or maybe..."

Peter gripped the back of one of the chairs.

"Or maybe I loved her so much I couldn't be without her. Even in death."

"Improbable. There has never been a couple, no matter how successful or attached, on the same Charon."

"After all the bogus things I've seen today, I'd say there's a first time for everything," Peter retorted.

The Conductor left Peter to his own devices and scanned the room.

"I mean, how else would you explain it? Huh?" Peter called after it.

"I'm telling you. I'm here because I'm trying to get my wife back. It's just like in the wedding vows. Till death do us part, except not even then!"

"Yet you didn't remember her?"

The man waved the Conductor off with a groan and sat at the table.

"My heart remembered her."

He imagined the woman sitting opposite him. Just the thought let loose a parade of butterflies in his stomach.

"Remember to follow the memory exactly."

"I would if I could. I'm going with what feels natural."

The Conductor raised its hands in compliance and moved to the bar. Peter watched the candlelight reflect off the red wine. Inside, at the bottom, was a wedding ring. He couldn't see it but he knew it was there. He'd watched her find it in her glass when he'd been here in life. Watched her put it on. Watched his heart break.

"Will the woman remember being a part of the simulation?" Peter asked.

The Conductor leaned against the bar.

"She should not. Unless we deviate from the memory in which her mind will understand that this is separate than her time on Earth."

"Really?"

"That is why we must try to reenact the memory as precise as possible. Any deviation will not only reveal us to the Recognition Conductor but could also alarm the woman's consciousness as well."

"Right," Peter said.

A door, on the far side of the restaurant, opened to reveal the woman. She entered wearing a flowing jade dress that highlighted the fire in her hair. On her arm, an adonis with broad shoulders, a square jaw, and buzzed brown hair led her toward the table for two.

Peter gritted his teeth. Looking at the adonis was like seeing a picture of the man he wanted to be and a painful reminder of what he wasn't. Same hair color, same eyes, practically same face. Only difference was the physique and the obvious confidence in this man's stride. A walk Peter was sure would have looked comical on him.

The woman's joyful smile vanished as she approached the table.

"Peter? What're you doing here? You can't be here," she said.

Her voice teetered like a pot nearing its boiling point. The Adonis loomed behind her, cutting daggers at Peter. He worried the muscled giant might strike him.

"Uh, I know. I know I can't, but I wanted to tell you. I needed to tell you, that I love you more than anything in the world." Peter left his seat and dropped to one knee.

The woman's lips curled back in disgust.

"Peter, get up. Luke and I are here to have dinner. You can't do this," the woman said.

"I know what you're here to do. I couldn't live with myself if I didn't fight for you!"

"I didn't ask you to!" she snapped.

"Alright, psycho, show's over," Luke said, ready to charge forward, but was stopped by the woman's hand on his shoulder.

"Listen to me. We're on the Charon express, a train taking us to the afterlife. We're dead. This is just a memory. We both ended up on the same train because we're meant to be!" Peter rattled, holding up his ringed hand as a sign of proof.

The woman and adonis froze while the other customers turned their heads toward Peter in unison, a blue glow illuminating from their eyes. The Conductor hurried from the bar to the restaurant's center.

"You've deviated from the memory. We have to go," it said, pulling Peter from the chair.

He struggled to stay at the table, pushing the Conductor away and reaching for the still woman.

"Listen to me! I'm sorry. I'm sorry for everything I did. Amy, I love you. Amy!"

The Conductor pulled Peter across the table, shattering the wine bottle and glasses to the floor. A line of red liquid snaked its way toward them as they fled, bringing with it a ring. A ring that Luke had given Amy this night. When she'd decided to marry him and ruin Peter's chances at happiness forever.

The blue-eyed patrons stood and began marching toward them. Their eyes charging like the Conductor's cannon. The Conductor transformed its arm and blasted the ones closest to the kitchen doors. Their bodies shone a brilliant blue before erupting into thousands of neon sparks that dissipated in the air.

The fabricated customers shot their own blue beams in retaliation, coming uncomfortably close to clipping Peter's backside. The kitchen doors opened as they drew near to reveal another transition hall. The Conductor practically threw Peter inside before jumping in after.

The two fell into a living room with a plush tan couch at the center. In front of it lay a glass coffee table, a white rug, and a T.V.

As Peter stood, he came face to face with some thirty colored pictured frames placed on the wall in the shape of a rainbow. Above the rainbow photos were two names drawn in cursive.

Luke & Amy.

In each photo, a memory he never got to have. Memories that should have been his. Memories he'd seen before. The guilt came back a hundredfold. His hands turned cold and clammy. A sixth sense prickled the back of his spine, causing the hairs on his neck to stand. He didn't even hear the humming of blue energy gathering in the cannon until he turned to find the Acceptance Conductor pointing his transmogrified arm at him.

"You called her by name. How would you know her name?" it asked.

"I remembered in the moment."

"That is a lie."

"Yeah well I'm surprised I got this far, honestly. Never been a great liar."

Peter grabbed a frame, a picture of Amy in a flowing white dress, and rubbed it between his fingers like fine silk. Then, flung it across the room, and then another, and another, pelting picture after picture into the opposite wall. Each one shattered to the floor, gathering broken bits of colorful wood and glass in every corner of the room.

"I'm going to take this opportunity to remind you. I still have mixed feelings and will eradicate you," the Conductor warned, its weapon still trained.

"Like you even know how to feel, you tin-can bastard."

Peter threw one of the last pictures at the Conductor and raced to the back door only to find it impossibly locked from the outside. He tried the garage to his right, the same. The front door stood behind the Conductor, but instead of shooting him, the Conductor turned to the door and twisted the handle with its free hand. It didn't budge.

The only option left was the closet, which shared the same wall as the affronting rainbow collage. Peter's body shook with ragged breaths. He cocked his head toward the closet door and gently brought a hand above the round doorknob. Something between a laugh and a sob stifled in his throat.

"I don't want her to remember me like this," he mumbled.

"That is unavoidable."

"Just don't make me relive this one. Any one but this one," Peter whispered.

The Conductor's blue eye took on a puzzled expression.

"Ever since I woke up, I've felt this horrible shame, this guilt. When I saw Amy in that first cart, I thought I could fix it. Make it all right again. Be something more than the creepy ex-husband who follows her and her new boyfriend around. We were meant to be. I know we were. I feel like a real person when I'm with her. She made me better. That's what your partner is supposed to do, right?"

The Conductor did not answer.

"Can't we just skip this one?"

"I'm afraid we cannot. I have never failed my programming and do not intend to do so now. I will gather the necessary data on your life experience and present it to the Engineer."

Tears formed in Peter's eyes.

"Fine," he said.

His hand fell gently on the closet's round knob that, unlike its predecessors, opened with ease. Simultaneously, the front door flung open as well to reveal Amy and Luke in a passionate kiss. The fallen pictures repaired themselves and flew back to their place in the rainbow. The couple, intertwined in fiery embrace, traveled to the sofa, refusing to separate their lips for more than a second.

Peter watched the couple with a deadpan expression. Luke laid Amy down on the sofa, her hands clawing into his back as he drew a trail of kisses down her neck.

"I wonder how far they'll get," Peter said.

As if answering him, the couple froze.

"Where were you in this memory?" the Conductor asked.

Peter pointed to the closet door with his thumb.

The Conductor made a whizzing sound that Peter could only interpret as its version of a sigh.

"Then that is where we must go."

Peter backed away from the door in defiance.

"I'm not doing it. Just give me whatever placement you want."

The Conductor's blue circle peered into Peter's hollow eyes. Then dropped its cannon arm back into the form of a hand.

"Even if I offered you the same placement as her?" The Conductor said, opening the closet door fully to allow Peter to step inside.

"Can you do that?"

"I must observe the crucial moments of your life to prepare your placement. After that, I can speak to the Engineer on your behalf, ensuring that you and Amy receive the same placement."

Peter swallowed and ran a hand across his lips.

"How long do these memories usually last?"

"They vary depending on the situation being observed. Normally, they play until there is a resolution."

Peter began pacing the room like a caged animal. Spinning on his heels anytime he came too close to the couple locked in stasis.

"You're sure? No bullshit? You can promise we'll share the same placement?"

"I will do what I can."

The Conductor offered their hand slowly, its neon eye taking on the closest thing it could to pity.

Peter hesitated. What came next would be the worst of it. But if reliving it meant a chance to right his mistakes. A chance to be with Amy, be the man she deserved. He would do it.

The Conductor nodded down at its palm.

"We do not have long before we are discovered. Only the partial correctness of the closet door buys us time."

"Fine."

Peter clasped the Conductor's and followed him into the closet, where they returned the door to its cracked position.

On cue, Luke and Amy burst back into action. Peter groaned and closed his eyes.

"Did you hear that?" Amy asked, instinctively drawing her recently removed shirt to her chest.

"Yeah," Luke growled, getting up from the couch.

Peter let out a knowing exhale and waited while Luke searched the room like a jungle cat hunting its prey.

"You don't think someone is in the house, do you?" Amy asked.

"I think if they are, I'm about to kick their ass," Luke said, now heading straight for the closet that Peter and the Conductor hid in.

Amy grabbed his arm. "What if they found your gun?"

"Good. They'll have some protection."

Luke shook her off and opened the closet.

"I'm sorry! Amy, I'm sorry!" Peter said busting out the door.

Amy's shriek could have landed her a role in a horror film. Even Luke, with his impressive physical stature, nearly jumped out of his skin. His face flushed with embarrassment and anger. Well, mostly anger.

"I could have guessed," Luke said.

He charged Peter into the wall, holding him up by his red suit.

"How long you been in there, you little creep? Huh? How long!"

"Amy, I made a mistake, a huge mistake!" Peter said.

He did not fight back or struggle against Luke's grip. He knew what he must say in order to keep the memory spinning.

"A mistake? You broke into our house and spied on us by mistake?" Luke snapped.

Luke cracked Peter's head to the side with a right hook and pulled him back to a standing position. The side of Peter's face grew dark and swollen.

"Now tell me, sicko, how exactly do you do that by mistake?"

Another punch split Peter's lip.

"Huh? C'mon tell me?"

Peter spit out the blood pooling in his mouth. He found Luke's eyes and held him there. The one shred of solace for Peter was that he knew what was coming. Luke did not.

"Please don't hit me again," Peter droned.

"Oh we're beyond begging, creep!" Luke said before continuing his onslaught.

25

Each hit made Peter's world spin and his face erupt in fire.

"No. Luke, stop. That's enough!" Amy said.

Enraged, Luke drew his fist back even further than the last.

Amy ran over to the men and grabbed Luke's arm. He pushed her off and brought another blow to Peter's stomach. The Conductor stood by and watched.

Peter's dizziness overtook the pain. Just as he remembered, a fog enveloped his brain. He was hardly cognizant. Luke seemed to gain new vigor with each attack. His face appeared more animal than human.

"You're trash! You're nothing compared to me. You hear me? You're nothing!"

"Luke stop! Damn it, Luke! I said STOP!" Amy cried.

She pulled at him between punches, but he wouldn't listen.

"I said stop. Luke! I'll call the police, I swear. This isn't the way to do this. Just stop. Fucking stop!"

"Would you shut up!" Luke said, swinging his other fist around.

Amy crumbled to the ground, falling silently behind the couch. A roar rose in Peter's throat, the moment of distraction he'd waited for. Peter tackled Luke into the glass table behind him. There was a shattering sound, followed by a sickening moan. Peter struggled to lift himself, shards of glass jutting into his hands. Beneath him, Luke's body convulsed as a pool of red liquid spread across the white rug. A final breath escaped the adonis's lips before leaving his body still.

"Oh my god. Oh my god. Oh my god," Amy said.

Peter turned to see Amy's hands clawing into the carpet as she dragged herself from behind the couch. her face screwed up into a silent scream. She rushed to Luke's body, pushing Peter to the side. Peter rolled over onto the rest of the shards that littered the floor. If they cut into him, he did not feel it. The only thing he could focus on was her pain. The Conductor stepped over him.

"The memory has not concluded?" the Conductor questioned.

Peter kept his eyes on Amy and pointed to the wide-open front door.

"I see," the Conductor said and offered its hand.

Peter closed his fists around the glass in his palms. Jagged shards pierced his skin, producing thick drops of blood that joined with Luke's. This part would be the hardest to relive.

"If you can place us together. I need to know she'll be happy. That she won't remember what I did to her."

"I can only offer you the chance of being placed together. What you do with that placement is up to you," the Conductor said.

Peter lifted a hand.

"Okay. Let's get it over with."

The Conductor gingerly pulled Peter up by the wrists. They stumbled through the front door and onto a serene landscape, untouched by the events hidden inside the house. A ranch, illuminated by the orange incandescent glow, splayed out before them. Goosebumps spread across Peter's arms as he entered the midnight air. Everything was still except for a few crickets and the rustling of leaves. The outside hadn't noticed a thing, cold and apathetic to the man lying in a pool of his own blood or the woman who knelt above him. Grieving.

"Why has the memory not ended?" the Conductor asked.

"She hasn't gotten the gun yet," Peter said.

The Conductor turned its hood toward Peter. Its neon eye shrunken to the size of quarter.

From behind them, a scream pierced the night's silence. The two turned to find Amy clutching a gun in trembling hands. A deep purple circle on her right eye contrasted against her tan skin.

Peter pulled himself from the Conductor and walked towards her. The words behind his teeth made him sick, but he had to say them. It was what he'd said back then. He took a deep breath that trembled as it left him.

"Why don't you love me?"

Peter never felt the bullet, only the falling.

Seconds became eons as his body slowly drifted toward the ground. Every memory that made up his pathetic and dull life played in his mind as he fell. He was a nice guy, just one born with no particular talent. No exceptional quality that proved he was special. None but the fact that Amy had once agreed to marry him.

Finally, his fall ended except his back was not met by the hard ground but by a cushioned seat. A familiar stark and sterile scent invaded his nostrils. The Conductor sat across from him just like before.

"We have completed the recognition process," the Conductor said.

Peter sank into his chair.

"As programming dictates, we will now move to the engine room for your placement."

"Our deal still stands? Amy and I get to go to the beyond together?"

The Conductor nodded.

"You will be given the same placement," it said mutedly.

"Good," Peter said.

The Conductor's cowl twitched.

" I will first meet with the Engineer, alone, to explain the situation. Until then, you and Amy will wait here."

"She's here?"

The Conductor gestured to the door behind Peter. It opened as Amy stepped through.

"I won't be long," the Conductor said and disappeared behind the opposite door.

"Amy. Amy, I'm so sorry," Peter said, rushing over to meet her.

Her eyes were full of red cracks and her nostrils flared. She took a step to the side as he approached.

"Don't," she said.

"Don't what?"

"Don't say it, again. That you're sorry. You're not sorry."

"I am, though. I'm sorry for what happened with Luke. I just wanted to protect you. I love you, enough to fight for you no matter what. I mean, c'mon, we're on the same train traveling to the afterlife if that doesn't say meant to be then I don't know what does."

Amy shook her head and placed her hands to her stomach.

"You are not fighting for me, Peter."

"What're you talking about? Of course I am."

"No. You're not. If you were fighting for me and my happiness you would have thought about how I would've felt going through any of this. I just had to relive watching my husband die."

"A husband who hit you."

Amy pivoted on her feet and slammed a hand to her chest, her voice rising in both pitch and intensity.

"I didn't say he was perfect. I didn't say he was the right one, but I still had to watch him die. You made me watch that. Twice. You're so focused on being with me that you never take into consideration if I want to be with you."

The words doubled him over, stronger than any punch Luke had thrown.

"What're you saying? After all of this, I'm still not enough for you. I just made a deal with some space robot to make sure we could be together in eternity. What more can I do?" Peter shouted.

"Stop it! You can stop trying to run my life! You want to know why we didn't work, Peter? Because you never believed that I could love you and were so sure of it, you made me sure of it, too. You act like the world is against you but you never acknowledge when you fuck up! You don't love me. You love the person you think being with me makes you."

Amy didn't wait for a response. It was clear to Peter she didn't want one. She stormed past him and through the circular door that led to the Engineer. Leaving Peter to drift about the room in a haze.

"But I…" he muttered.

He found himself back at the wall where he'd accidentally discovered the window. He opened it. Outside, the cosmos had shifted.

He asked the stars, "What do I have to do to be happy with the man I am?" What do I have to do to get rid of this guilt?"

The stars offered only silence along with the reflection of his own face against the window.

Eventually, Peter pressed the touchscreen again and headed for the circular door. Everything was the same as before except for the addition of Amy who stood beside the Conductor. Peter joined them but said nothing.

"It's time for the placement," the Conductor said.

It moved between the humans, putting Peter on the left and Amy on the right. Like before, the panels on the Conductor's chest retreated behind their torso to reveal the glowing blue crystal beneath. The crystal reached out with its blue arcing light, connecting itself to the fiery body of the Engineer.

"I will relay the Engineer's decision to you both. The placement begins."

Two portals, the size of semi-trucks, opened before the Charon's front window. To the right, hovered a light blue oval portal spiraling inward. On the left, a mirrored portal of fire.

"Amy Francis Sanders will be placed first."

Amy instinctively took a step forward, keeping her eyes trained on the Engineer and notably away from Peter.

"Amy. You have faced Recognition, come to Acceptance, and will now receive placement."

Every being with the lungs to do so, held their breath. A second, possibly the longest one in the two earthlings history passed by at a trudging pace. Another heat wave radiated from the Engineer. When it passed over Amy, her body became shrouded in glittering orange particles.

"No!" Peter whispered.

Amy wrapped her arms around herself and nodded as a tremor ran down her spine. Tears formed at the corners of her eyes but she refused them, flinging them away with her fingertips. She threw her head back, puffed out her chest, and slowly crossed to the orange portal.

Peter swayed, his feet barely catching his weight. He rushed forward and grabbed Amy by the arm.

"Can she stay just to see my placement!" he cried out.

The Conductor's blue circle went through a myriad of shapes and sizes.

"Would you allow this, Engineer?" it asked.

The orb modulated in the air.

"Allowed," the Conductor said. Its robotic voice could not suppress its surprise.

Amy's gawked at Peter. He smiled and squeezed her arm before taking his position in front of the Engineer.

"Peter Michael Dumont. You have faced Recognition, come to Acceptance, and will now receive placement."

The Engineer emitted its decisive energy once more. An orange mist clung to Peter's body.

Peter cocked his head, immediately saying, "Knew it. Thank you Godlike being, sir. If it's all right with you, I'd like to walk in with Amy. I don't want her to face this alone."

The Conductor's circle shrunk to the size of a quarter and expanded back out again.

"Engineer?"

It was hard to tell without a face, but the orb seemed to turn to Peter, as much as an orb can turn. The Engineer expanded several inches and shrunk again, releasing a gentle summer breeze.

"Roughly translating...Why not?" said the Conductor.

Peter clapped his hands together. Amy's eyebrows attempted to fly off her face and into the sky like a child's lost balloon. He returned to her side and took her by the arm, seemingly ignoring the blatant confusion that overtook her countenance. They continued their bewildered march toward the gateway of promised punishment.

"Trust me?" Peter mouthed now that their backs were turned to their non-mortal observers.

Amy squeezed his hand in protest but played along. They were close. A few yards from the bright veil of molten energy. They could feel the insurmountable heat already threatening to blister their skin. The blue portal stood just a few yards away. Almost... Almost...Now!

Peter yanked Amy's arm and shoved her toward the blue portal. Amy stumbled forward, mere inches away.

her hand reached out and pierced the vortex. A strange vacuuming sound rang through the chamber as Amy's body was sucked in.

"Peter!" Amy's voice echoed.

"Yes!" Peter screamed, throwing two triumphant fists into the air.

The entire Charon shook as the Engineer spun and morphed its spherical shape at an alarming rate. The rumbling threw Peter to the ground.

"What have you done?" the Conductor said.

"I have no idea, but I'm pretty sure it was finally the right thing!" Peter said, still scrambling to right himself.

The Engineer produced a fire whip from its body and cracked it in the air. The whip circled the room before returning for Peter, who threw his arms up in defense.

"Wait!" the Conductor called.

The blue line between it and the Engineer wavered emphatically. The whip paused mere inches from Peter's face.

"I call for a reevaluation," the Conductor said.

The orb shifted in the Conductor's direction. Then slowly drew its death whip back inch by terrifying inch.

"I have observed the subject, Peter Dumont, and find that they have not only recognized their enormities, but through a want of reconciliation have acted in the best interest of their victim with no promise of reward. Therefore, I offer the conclusion that this is a deed deserving of reevaluation."

The Conductor had spoken so fast that Peter's eyes went blank trying to process. The Engineer bobbed erratically. When it was done communicating what Peter could only imagine were rather unkind things, the Conductor spread its arms and continued the debate.

"Precisely. They have defied the workings of the system, and in that action compromised what we knew of the system's function. Their intelligence, though limited—"

"Hey!" Peter interjected from his knees.

"—though limited, is adequate enough to compute that their recent action would lead to their destruction. Revealing it to be a selfless act. An act we did not observe during their time alive. Therefore, they must have fundamentally changed and thus must be reevaluated as a new subject."

The Engineer grew still then floated up and down as if nodding to the Conductor. The Conductor's blue eye turned to a half circle. Its arms drifted toward to their sides. Whatever the Engineer had said, it had greatly affected them.

"I understand and I accept. I will stake my existence on the results of their reevaluation."

The Engineer let out a blast of energy and the two portals disappeared, a white portal appearing in their stead.

"You'll do what?" Peter asked, still kneeling.

"If you do not prove to be better in your second life, I will be terminated."

"I thought you had mixed feelings about me?"

"That circumstance has not changed."

Peter chortled and cried simultaneously.

"I can't hug you because you got that blue line thing which I'm sure would kill me but just know I would."

The Conductor titled their metallic cowl.

"I merely request you live this life differently than the last."

"You got it chief," Peter said with a playful salute before turning to the Engineer, "Your scariness."

Peter's walk turned to a run by the time he vanished into the white portal. The moment he crossed the threshold, it collapsed and the blue line between Conductor and Engineer retracted. The Conductor moved to the space the white portal had occupied and felt the air in front of them with their hand. The Engineer pulsed indignantly behind them.

"There is a high probability you are correct, but just as my programming was not invariable, neither, do I believe, is his."

The compromised but no less indignant Engineer buzzed and crackled in what we can only guess was a vicious attempt at rudeness.

"Let us move to more productive matters. I propose the addition of a new section of the Charon."

Another pulse.

"Redemption." the Conductor said.

About the Author

Dylan Ritch is a writer with experience in film, stage, and education. Ritch is devoted to stories that settle in the hearts of his readers and hopes that in-between his pages readers will find laughter, reflection, and worlds beyond our own.

"When someone sits at a coffeeshop with a friend, apologizing profusely for ranting for over an hour about a book, I would be honored and grateful if that book turned out to be mine."

—Dylan Ritch

Other Books by Ritch

You can view Dylan's other works at
www.arrowheartpublishing.com
and on their Amazon Author page.

www.ingramcontent.com/pod-product-compliance
Lightning Source LLC
Chambersburg PA
CBHW020609130626
46552CB00007B/3127